This book belongs to:

....

Note to parents and carers

Read it yourself is a series of classic, traditional tales, written in a simple way to give children a confident and successful start to reading.

Each book is carefully structured to include many high-frequency words that are vital for first reading. The sentences on each page are supported closely by pictures to help with reading, and to offer lively details to talk about.

The books are graded into four levels that progressively introduce wider vocabulary and longer stories as a reader's ability grows.

Ideas for use

- Begin by looking through the book and talking about the pictures. Has your child heard this story before?

- Help her with any words she does not know, either by helping her to sound them out or supplying them yourself.

- Developing readers can be concentrating so hard on the words that they sometimes don't fully grasp the meaning of what they're reading. Answering the puzzle questions on pages 30 and 31 will help with understanding.

For more information and advice, visit www.ladybird.com/readityourself

Level 2 is ideal for children who have received some reading instruction and can read short, simple sentences with help.

Special features:

Frequent repetition of main story words and phrases

Short, simple sentences

Large, clear type

Careful match between story and pictures

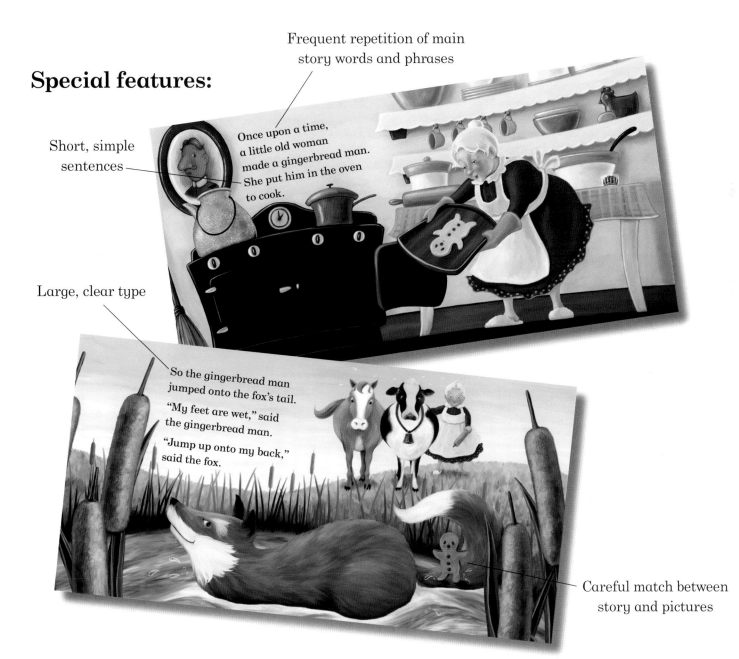

Once upon a time, a little old woman made a gingerbread man. She put him in the oven to cook.

So the gingerbread man jumped onto the fox's tail.

"My feet are wet," said the gingerbread man.

"Jump up onto my back," said the fox.

Educational Consultant: Geraldine Taylor

A catalogue record for this book is available from the British Library

Published by Ladybird Books Ltd
80 Strand, London, WC2R 0RL
A Penguin Company

004-10 9 8 7 6 5 4
© LADYBIRD BOOKS LTD MMX
Ladybird, Read It Yourself and the Ladybird Logo are registered or
unregistered trade marks of Ladybird Books Limited.

ISBN: 978-1-40930-358-9

Printed in China

The Gingerbread Man

Illustrated by Virginia Allyn

Once upon a time,
a little old woman
made a gingerbread man.
She put him in the oven
to cook.

6

Soon, the gingerbread man was cooked. The little old woman took him out of the oven.

The gingerbread man jumped up and ran out of the door.

"Stop, little gingerbread man!" shouted the little old woman.

"I want to eat you for my tea."

But the gingerbread man would not stop.

The little old woman chased the gingerbread man, but she could not catch him.

Soon, the gingerbread man met a cow.

"Stop, little gingerbread man!" shouted the cow.

"I want to eat you for my tea."

But the gingerbread man would not stop.

The cow chased the gingerbread man, but she could not catch him.

17

Soon, the gingerbread man met a horse.

"Stop, little gingerbread man!" shouted the horse.

"I want to eat you for my tea."

But the gingerbread man would not stop.

The horse chased the gingerbread man, but he could not catch him.

Soon, the gingerbread man came to a river. There he met a fox.

"I will help you to cross the river," said the fox. "Jump up onto my tail."

So the gingerbread man jumped onto the fox's tail.

"My feet are wet," said the gingerbread man.

"Jump up onto my back," said the fox.

So the gingerbread man
jumped onto the fox's back.

"My feet are still wet,"
said the gingerbread man.

"Jump up onto my head,"
said the fox.

So the gingerbread man
jumped onto the fox's head.

Snap! went the fox.
And that was the end of
the gingerbread man.

How much do you remember about the story of The Gingerbread Man? Answer these questions and find out!

- Who made the gingerbread man?

- Can you remember two of the animals the gingerbread man met?

- Why does the gingerbread man stop running?

- Who carries the gingerbread man over the river?

Look at the pictures and match them to the story words.

old woman

cow

fox

gingerbread man

Read it yourself
with Ladybird

The Three Billy Goats Gruff — Level 1

Cinderella — Level 1

Little Red Hen — Level 1

Goldilocks and the Three Bears — Level 1

The Magic Porridge Pot — Level 1

The Ugly Duckling — Level 1

The Gingerbread Man — Level 2

Sleeping Beauty — Level 2

Sly Fox and Red Hen — Level 2

The Three Little Pigs — Level 2

Town Mouse and Country Mouse — Level 2

Little Red Riding Hood — Level 2

The Elves and the Shoemaker — Level 3

Jack and the Beanstalk — Level 3

The Pied Piper of Hamelin — Level 4

The Wizard of Oz — Level 4

Collect all the titles in the series.